Rumble, Rumble, BOOM!

To Kayla Anne,
Enjoy the Music!
Daniella L. Muller

by

Daniella L. Muller

AuthorHouse™
1663 Liberty Drive
Bloomington, IN 47403
www.authorhouse.com
Phone: 1-800-839-8640

First published by AuthorHouse 10/15/2009

ISBN: 978-1-4389-7710-2 (sc)

Printed in the United States of America
Bloomington, Indiana

This book is printed on acid-free paper.

authorHOUSE®

For my two little bunnies, Alexis and Tommy
I Love You-
Mommy

It was bedtime at the Bunny house. Nibble Bunny had taken her tubby and brushed her teeth, and Papa Bunny had just finished reading her favorite book, *All About Carrots,* to her.

Mama and Papa Bunny kissed Nibble's soft, furry nose, turned out the lights, and said, "Sweet dreams, little bunny."

Nibble snuggled up under her covers with her special blankie and said, "Sweet dreams," as Mama and Papa Bunny closed her bedroom door.

Just as Nibble Bunny closed her eyes, she heard a loud noise coming from outside. She jumped up to look out the window, and then held her blankie close as she listened to the sound:

SSHHH Crackle … Rumble, Rumble, BOOM!
SSHHH Crackle … Rumble, Rumble, BOOM!

Nibble was shaking! She didn't like the loud noises she was hearing, and she wondered how she was possibly going to be able to sleep. She listened again:

SSHHH Crackle ... Rumble, Rumble, BOOM!

SSHHH Crackle ... Rumble, Rumble, BOOM!

Nibble called for Mama and Papa Bunny as she hopped out of bed. She was too scared to stay in bed for another minute!

"What is it, Nibble?" Papa Bunny said as he hurried into her room.

"What is that loud *RUMBLE* and *BOOM* sound outside my window?" Nibble asked. "I don't like that loud noise!"

Papa Bunny picked up little Nibble and sat her on her bed. He put his arm around her and explained, "There's a rainstorm outside, and sometimes when it rains … it thunders. The loud sound that you hear is thunder."

"What is thunder, Papa Bunny?" Nibble asked.

Papa Bunny looked out the window and said, "When you look out your window during a thunderstorm, you'll sometimes see a quick flash of light in the sky. That's called lightning. And thunder is the loud sound that lightning makes as it moves through the air."

"Did you like the loud thunder when you were a little bunny?" Nibble asked Papa Bunny.

Papa Bunny tucked Nibble under her covers, then snuggled close to her and said, "I remember when I was a little bunny, the thunder would scare me too."

"And what did you do, Papa Bunny?" Nibble asked.

"Grandpa Bunny would come into my room, tuck me back into bed, and tell me that thunder is the sound that the clouds make when they're playing their instruments in the sky!" Papa Bunny said.

"What kind of instruments?" asked Nibble.

"Drums, trumpets, cymbals—all kinds of instruments playing music just for you," said Papa Bunny.

"And when I was a little bunny, Grandpa Bunny would sit on my bed during a thunderstorm, and we would try to guess which songs the clouds were playing," Papa Bunny said. "What song do you think they're playing tonight?" he asked Nibble.

Papa Bunny and Nibble snuggled close and waited quietly for the next thunder to come.

SSHHH Crackle ... Rumble, Rumble, BOOM!

SSHHH Crackle ... Rumble, Rumble, BOOM!

Just then, Mama Bunny walked into the bedroom.

"What are you two doing in here?" Mama Bunny asked.

"We're listening to the music, Mama Bunny!" Nibble said as she jumped up excitedly.

"Oh!" said Mama Bunny giggling.

"Were you scared of thunder when you were a little bunny?" Nibble asked Mama Bunny.

"Yes, I remember being afraid of thunder when I was a little bunny. Grandma Bunny would remind me that just because a noise is loud doesn't mean it has to be scary," Mama Bunny explained as she walked over to Nibble's bed. "I bet I can think of lots of loud noises that you like!"

"Which loud noises, Mama Bunny?" Nibble asked.

"Well … let's see …," Mama Bunny said. "Making Popcorn! That makes a loud POP, POP, POP sound. And I know you love the taste of popcorn!" Mama Bunny smiled.

Nibble looked over at Papa Bunny and said, "What loud noises do you like?"

"Banging on a drum!" he said. "THUMP, THUMP, THUMP! Even though drums make a loud noise, it's fun to bang on them and make music!"

"And choo-choo trains pulling into the station. TOOT! TOOT! TOOT! Remember when we went on the train and met the conductor?" Papa Bunny asked Nibble.

But before Nibble could answer, Papa Bunny thought of *another* loud noise he liked! "Garbage trucks picking up the trash in the morning! EERRR ... SCREECH! When you were a little bunny, you would anxiously wait by the window for the garbage truck to arrive!" Papa Bunny said.

"I know a loud noise that I really like," Nibble said excitedly. "Fireworks on the 4th of July!

BOOM! BOOM! BOOM! And they make the most beautiful colors in the sky! Do you think the clouds like watching the fireworks?" she asked.

"I bet they do!" said Papa Bunny.

"Mama Bunny, what loud noises do you like?" Nibble asked.

"When I pretend that your belly is a carrot and I go, 'Crunch, crunch, crunch,' and I get to hear your loudest belly laugh!" Mama Bunny said as she pretended to nibble on Nibble's belly.

Nibble giggled loudly!

"All right, Nibble, it's time to go to sleep," said Papa Bunny. "I think I hear the clouds playing a rock-and-roll version of 'Twinkle, Twinkle, Little Star,' my favorite goodnight song," Papa Bunny said with a smile.

As Mama and Papa Bunny tucked Nibble into bed again, Nibble said, "Tomorrow morning, I'll tell you all the different instruments I hear the clouds playing tonight."

"Sweet music in the sky, Nibble!" whispered Mama and Papa Bunny.

Nibble's sleepy eyes begin to close as she drifts off to sleep.

Zzzz...

...Zzzz...

...Zzzz

Zzzz...

...Zzzz...

...Zzzz

LaVergne, TN USA
16 December 2009
167215LV00004B